Anthology

content provided
by Houghton Mifflin Harcourt
Supplemental Publishers, Inc.

Photo Acknowledgements: P.112 ©HMH Collection; p.119 ©HMH Collection; p.151 ©Kaz Mori/Image Bank/Getty Images; p.152.©Corel Royalty Free; p.153 ©Comstock; p.154 ©SuperStock; p.155 ©Michael Newman/PhotoEdit; p.156 ©Pictor Images/Imagestate; p.157 ©Alan Detrick/Photo Researchers, Inc.; p.158 ©Kaz Mori/Image Bank/Getty Images; P.201 (joey) ©Dave King/DK Images; p.201 (polar bear) ©Ken Graham/Getty Images; p.201 (crocodile, ducks) ©PhotoDisc/Getty Images; p.202 (duck) ©Barrie Watts/DK Images; p.202 (duckling) ©PhotoDisc/Getty Images; p.202 (kangaroo) ©CORBIS; p.203 (polar bears) ©Norbert Rosing/Getty Images; p.203 (crocodile w/egg) ©Jonathan Blair/CORBIS; p.203 (crocodile) ©PhotoDisc/Getty Images; p.209 (bgd) ©HMH Collection; p.209 (girl) ©Bob Krist/CORBIS; p.210 ©Owen Franken/CORBIS; p.211 ©Comstock; p.217 ©PictureQuest; p.218 ©Martin B. Withers/CORBIS; p.219 (tadpole) ©Oxford Scientific Films/Animals Animals; p.219 (gills) ©GaryMeszaros/Photo Researchers, Inc.; p.219 (legs) ©Hans Pfletschinger/Peter Arnold, Inc.; p.219 (frog) ©David A. Northcott/CORBIS; p.225 (wheelchair race) ©Jim Cummins/Getty Images; p.225 (apple) ©SuperStock; p.226 ©PhotoDisc/Getty Images; p.228 (germs) ©S. Lowry/Univ. Ulster/Getty Images; p.228 (microscope) ©PhotoDisc/Getty Images; p.228 (washing) ©EyeWire/Getty Images; p.233 (parade) ©Ariel Skelley/CORBIS; p.233 (Kwanzaa) ©CORBIS; p.233 (girls) ©Don Tremain/Photodisc/Getty Images Royalty Free; p.234 ©Fulvio Roiter/CORBIS; p.235 (ice sculpture) ©Getty Images; p.235 (canoe race) Courtesy of Frederic Lavoie/ Quebec Winter Carnaval; p.236 (spring) ©AFP/CORBIS; p.236 (summer) ©Chris Lisle/CORBIS;

All assignment photography ©Alan Landau.

Additional photography by Comstock Royalty Free; ImageState Royalty Free; Photos.com Royalty Free; Photodisc/Getty Royalty Free; PictureQuest Royalty Free and Royalty-Free/CORBIS.

ISBN 1-4190-2658-5

Printed in the United States of America
8 9   1420   14 13 12 11
4500339093

Contents

Level A

Phonics

Contents

Comprehension

THE PAN MAN

WRITTEN BY MARK DAY

Sam can wash the pans.

Sam can play with the pans.

What can Sam make?

Sam stacks the pans.

Sam adds hot pads and a rag.

Sam adds a hat last.

Sam has made a pan man.

Sam can be a pan man, too!

Act Like a Cat

Written by Mark Day

Illustrated by Pamela Paparone

Maggie is a black cat.

Danny is her pal.

Maggie can act like a dog.

Maggie can wag her tail for Danny.

Maggie can catch a ball from Danny.

Maggie can dance for Danny.

But when Danny goes to school, . . .

Maggie acts like a cat!

Ten Cents

Written by Linda Lott

I have ten cents.
What can I get?

Can I get the hen?
Yes! You bet I can!

Now I have six cents!
What can I get?

Can I get the jet?
Yes! You bet I can!

I have just three cents left.
What can I get?

Can I get the red pen?
Yes! You bet I can!

I have a hen, a jet, and a pen.

I still have two cents left!
What else can I get?

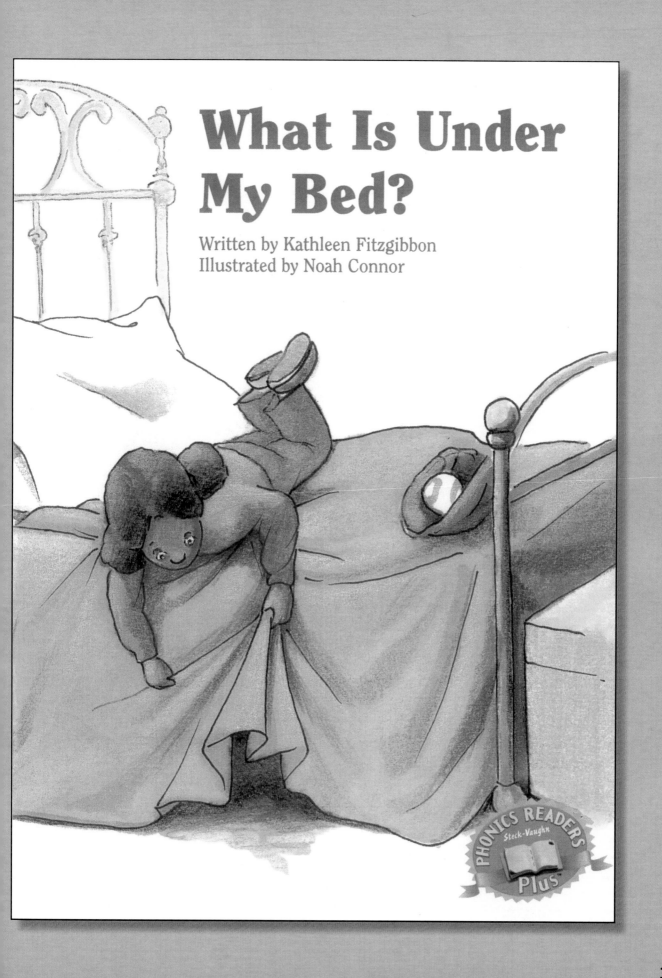

What Is Under My Bed?

Written by Kathleen Fitzgibbon
Illustrated by Noah Connor

What is that?
How did it get under my bed?

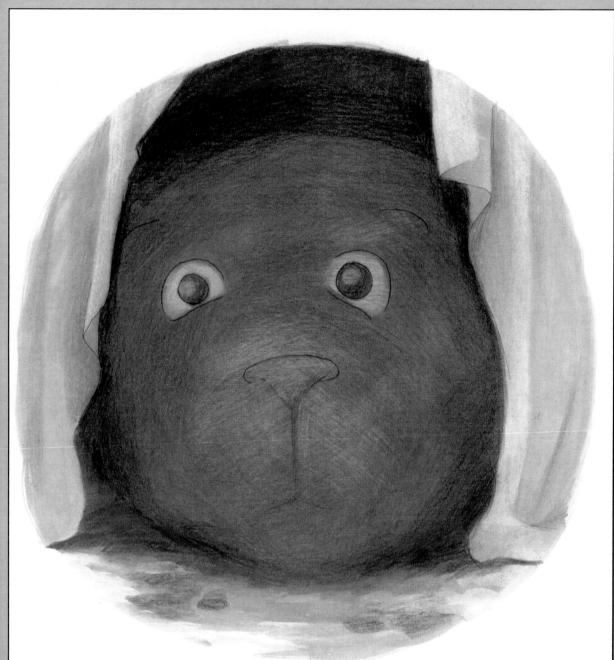

Is it wet?
Yes, it is wet.
How did it get under my bed?

Is it a mess?
Yes, it is a mess.
How did it get under my bed?

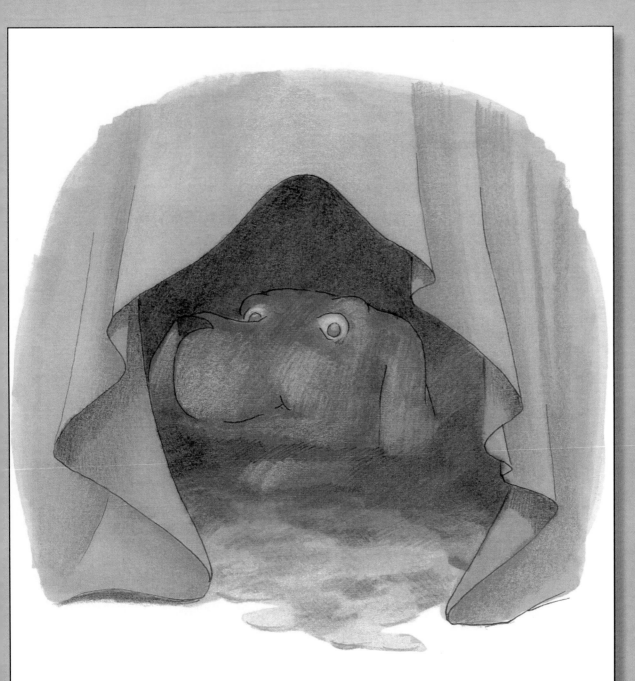

Is it red?
Yes, it is red.
How did it get under my bed?

Does it have legs?
Yes, it has legs.
How did it get under my bed?

Is it my pet?
Yes, it is my pet.
How did my pet get under my bed?

Is it Rex?
Yes, it is Rex.
How did Rex get under my bed?

Rex is all wet.
He is a big mess!

Kim's Wish

Written by Carolyn Crimi
Illustrated by Deborah Morse

Kim has a little pig.
His name is Skinny.
Kim wishes Skinny could play.

All Skinny does is
sit . . .

      and *sit* . . .

           and *sit*.

Kim wears a silly wig.
She dips and spins.
Kim wishes Skinny could spin, too.

All Skinny does is
sit . . .

and *sit* . . .

and *sit*.

Kim gets some chips.
Then she sips some milk.
Kim wishes Skinny could sip, too.

All Skinny does is
sit . . .

      and *sit* . . .

            and *sit*.

Kim slips into bed.
She hugs Skinny.
Soon Kim is asleep.
Will Skinny sit and sit?

Skinny winks and grins.
Then HE gives Kim a big hug, too!

What Is Missing?

Written by Mark Day

Kim and Jill will fix lunch.
They pick chips and dip.
They pick tuna fish and carrot sticks.

Jill gets the can of tuna fish.
She mixes it in a dish.
Kim adds pickle bits to the dish.

Kim gets two big glasses.
Jill fills each glass with milk.
They will have milk with their tuna fish.

Kim unzips a bag of chips.
She puts the chips in a big dish.
Jill whips up the thick dip.

Jill gets six carrot sticks.
They are thin and crisp.
Kim puts the carrot sticks on a plate.

Jill and Kim sit down to eat
"It is time to eat a bit," says Kim.
"But something is missing."

The chips are missing!
"Let's find Jim," says Jill.
"I bet he hid the chips."

"There he is!" says Jill.
"Look at his grin."
Jim ate all the chips!

Hop, Hop, Hop

Written by Leya Roberts

Illustrated by Esther Szegedy

PHONICS READERS
Steck-Vaughn
Plus

Rob sees Frog hop.
Rob can hop, too.

Hop, hop, hop.
Frog hops on a log.

Rob can hop, too.
He hops on the log.

Hop, hop, hop.
Frog hops on a rock.

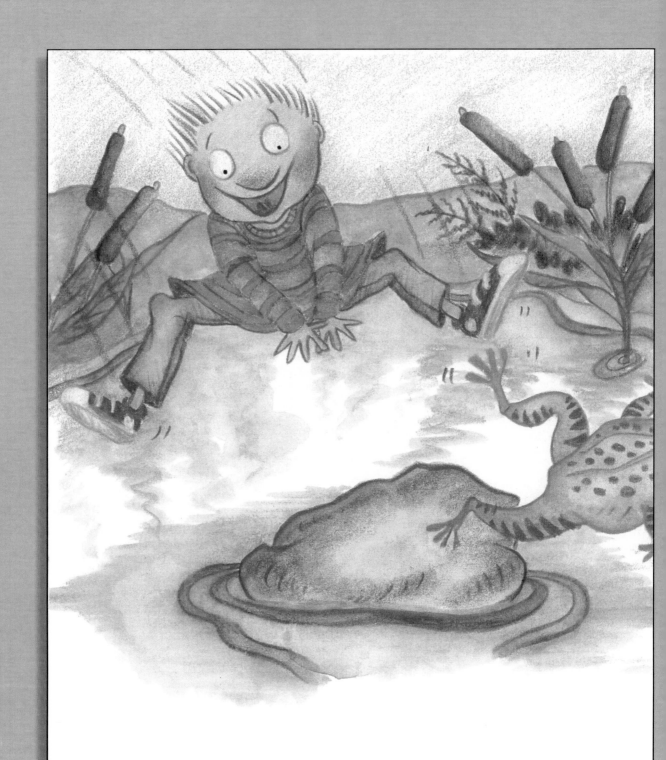

Rob can hop, too.
He hops on the rock.

Hop, hop, hop.
Frog hops to a pond.

Rob can hop, too.
He hops to the pond.

Rob stops!
He cannot hop ON a pond!

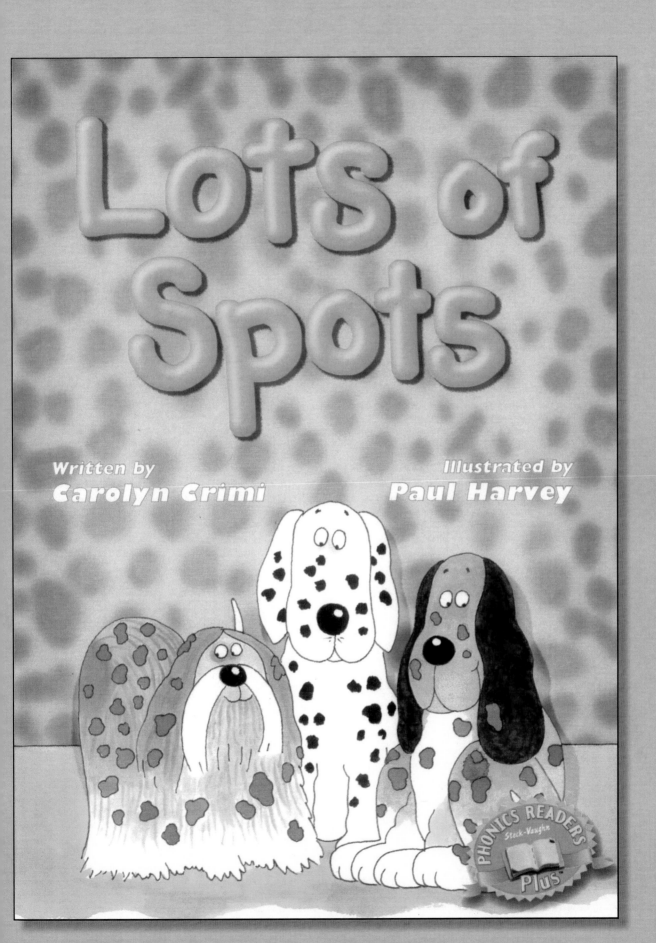

Lots of Spots

Written by
Carolyn Crimi

Illustrated by
Paul Harvey

PHONICS READERS
Steck-Vaughn
Plus

Moppy has a spot.

Floppy has a few spots.

Dottie has lots of spots.

Moppy and Floppy want more spots.

Dottie dips a mop in paint.

Dottie drops spots on top of Moppy.
Plop,

plop,

plop.

Dottie drops spots on top of Floppy.
Plop,
          plop,
                  plop.

Now Moppy and Floppy have
lots
      of
           spots!

Mud Is So Much Fun!

Written by Leya Roberts
Illustrated by Carol O'Malia

Cubby Bear likes the mud.
Mud is so much fun!

82

Cubby Bear runs in a big mud puddle. Mud is so much fun!

Cubby Bear jumps in the mud.
Mud is so much fun!

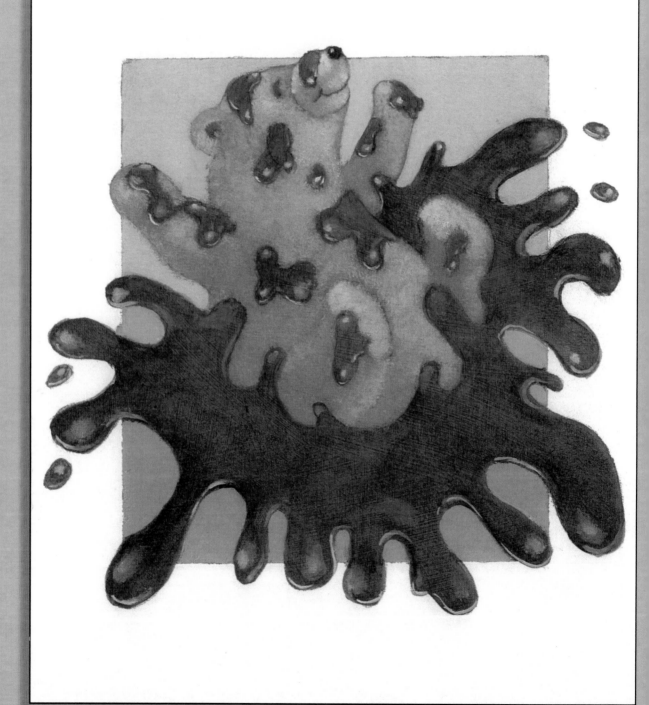

Cubby Bear sits in the mud.
Mud is so much fun!

Cubby Bear rolls in the mud.
Mud is so much fun!

Cubby Bear sees Fuzzy Bear.
He gets up and runs to her.

Cubby Bear gives Fuzzy Bear a hug.
His big bear hug gets mud on her.

Mud is so much fun.
But it is not for hugs!

Gus Is Such a Funny Bug!

Written by Kathleen Fitzgibbon
Illustrated by Patrick Girouard

Gus is just a bug.
But he moves in such funny ways.

Gus has a pink and yellow umbrella.
It lifts him up and up.
He is such a funny bug.

Gus has suds under his tub.
His tub is a rub-a-dub sub.
He is such a funny bug.

Gus jumps in mud.
He gets stuck in a rut.
He is such a funny bug.

Gus has a fuzzy coat.
He wears it to swim in the sun.
He is such a funny bug.

Gus flies upside down.
Gus crunches and munches on nuts.
He is such a funny bug.

Gus naps in his upper bunk.
He hugs his rubber ducks.
He is such a funny bug.

Gus is such a funny bug!

Jamie's Play

Written by Mark Day

PHONICS READERS
Steck-Vaughn
Plus

My name is Jamie.
I will be in a play.
The play is about a lion and a mouse.

I am the brave lion.
I am tame.
I have a very big mane.

I see the face of a gray mouse.
I see the tail of the mouse, too.
I yell, "The mouse scares me!"

I run this way.
The mouse races the same way.
Why does he chase me?

We race and race across the stage.
I wish the mouse would stay away.
This is not a game.

The mouse steps on my tail.
I shake my mane.
I am a brave lion.

The gray mouse takes off his mask.
He shows his face.
The mouse is my pal Jay!

The play is over.
Jay takes my hand.
We will bow and wave.

The Amazing Kate

Written by Elizabeth Sengel
Illustrated by Priscilla Burris

Kate plays all day long.
Now it is time to take a nap.
She dreams that she is Amazing Kate.

Kate dreams . . .

She is by the lion cage.
She plays a soft song.
She makes the lion tame.

Kate dreams . . .

She has a cape.
She has a hat and cane, too.
She taps her way across the stage.

Kate dreams . . .

She sails on the bay.
She races on the waves.
She is brave and safe.

Kate dreams . . .

She puts on her skates.
She spins around in one place.
She has a big smile on her face.

Kate dreams . . .

She hits the baseball.
She runs the bases.
She helps her team win the game.

Kate dreams . . .

She sees a train go the wrong way.
It is as fast as a plane.
She makes the train go the right way.

Kate wakes up.
It is Amazing Kate!
What else can she do today?

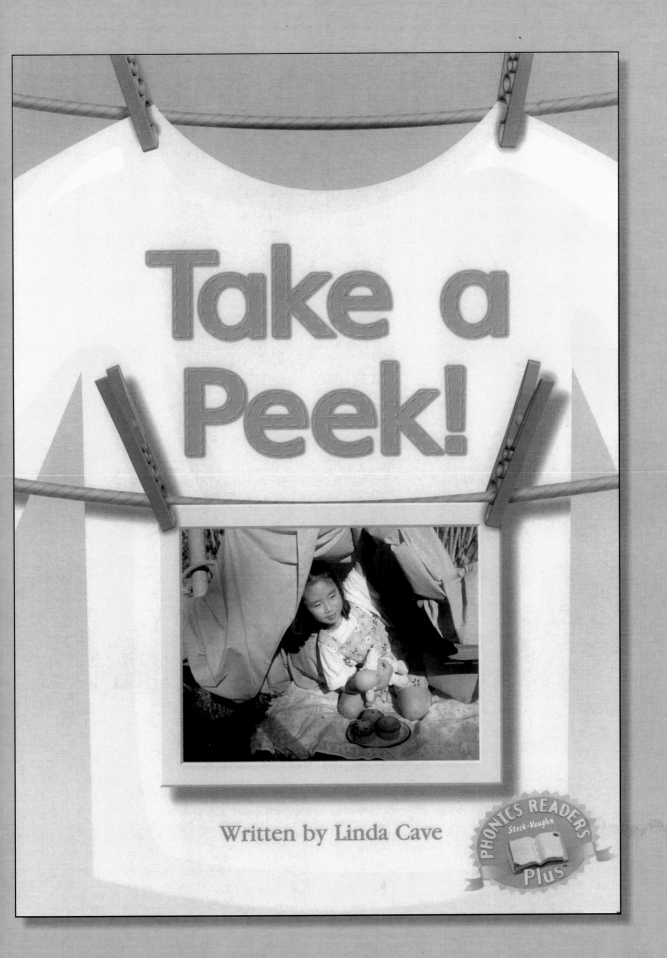

Take a Peek!

Written by Linda Cave

PHONICS READERS
Steck-Vaughn
Plus

Lee sees a clean sheet.
The sheet seems to fly.

The sheet is just what Lee needs.
She takes two seats to the sheet.

Lee pulls the sheet over the seats.
The sheet will make a pretty tent!

Lee will eat a treat in the tent.
"I will keep my tent clean," she says.

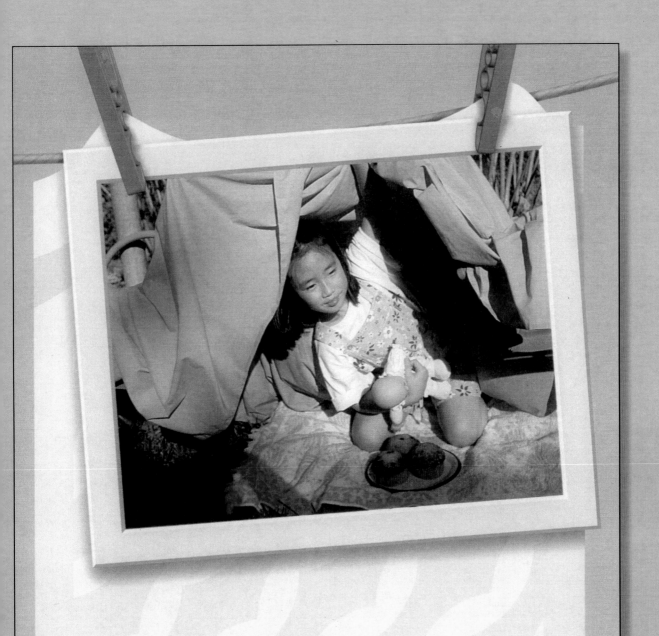

Lee peeks from the sheet.
"What a neat place for me," says Lee.

Teeny sees Lee in the tent.
Teeny sees a treat, too.

EeK! Teeny tugs the sheet.
The sheet falls on Lee.

Lee says, "Now, I know what I can be.
I will keep the sheet on me.
I can be a queen!"

Baby Bee

Written by Elizabeth Sengel
Illustrated by Paul Borovsky

This is the Bee family.
Meet Mama Bee and Papa Bee.
Meet Baby Bee, too.

Mama Bee is a busy bee.
Papa Bee is a busy bee.
Baby Bee is a tiny bee.

Baby Bee has many big dreams.
She wants to be more than a tiny bee.
She dreams about what she can be.

Baby Bee may be a speedy bee.
She will swim in the deep blue sea.
She will ride on the back of a seal.

Baby Bee may be a breezy bee.
She will fly up into the sky.
She will leave a long green streak.

Baby Bee may be a chilly bee.
She will reach the tallest peak.
She will think it was not steep.

Baby Bee may be a jumpy bee.
She will leap over the moon.
She will land on her feet.

But now, Baby Bee is a sleepy bee.
Sweet dreams to Baby Bee.

Mike Likes Stripes

Written by Linda Cave
Illustrated by Bethann Thornburgh

PHONICS READERS
Steck-Vaughn
Plus

Mike likes stripes.
His bike has stripes.
His kite has stripes.
Mike says stripes are nice.

Spike likes stripes, too.
His coat has stripes.
His house has stripes.
Spike says stripes are nice.

Mike likes stripes at home.
His room has stripes.
His bed has stripes.
Mike says stripes are nice.

Mike likes stripes for dress up.
His tie has stripes.
His suit has stripes.
Mike says stripes are nice.

Mike likes stripes at school.
His book has stripes.
His desk has stripes.
Mike says stripes are nice.

Mike likes stripes at lunch.
His cookie has stripes.
His lunch box has stripes.
Mike says stripes are nice.

Mike likes stripes at the zoo.
The fish have stripes.
The birds have stripes.
Mike says stripes are nice.

Even the tiger has stripes.
The tiger growls at Mike.
Yipes!
These stripes may NOT be nice!

JoJo's Road Trips

Written by Dennis Fertig
Illustrated by Karen Dugan

JoJo the Goat has an old red truck.
She takes big loads on the road.

This load has roses and soap.
JoJo takes the load to Rosie.

"Thanks, JoJo," says Rosie the Skunk.
"I like things that smell good."

This load has notes and a phone.
JoJo takes the load to Bo.
"Thanks, JoJo," says Bo the Snake.
"Now I will not feel so alone."

This load has hats and coats.
JoJo takes the load to Homer.
"Thanks, JoJo," says Homer the Mole.
"It gets cold in my home."

This load has boats and ropes.
JoJo takes the load to Goldie.
"Thanks, JoJo," says Goldie the Fish.
"I like things that float."

This is the last load.
It has a roast and a loaf of bread.

JoJo takes this load home.
"Home, sweet home," says JoJo.

Tony's Yellow Boat

Written by Gail Blasser Riley

Illustrated by Ken Bowser

Tony has a yellow boat.

Tony hopes his boat can float.

Tony hopes his boat can float
with a note from Joe.

Tony hopes his boat can float
with a note from Joe
            and a doggie bone.

Tony hopes his boat can float
with a note from Joe, a doggie bone,
and a long red rose.

Tony hopes his boat can float
with a note from Joe, a doggie bone,
    a long red rose, and a bar of soap.

Tony hopes his boat can float
with a note from Joe, a doggie bone,
a long red rose, a bar of soap,
and a tiny toy toad.

Tony's boat with the note, the bone,
the rose, the soap, and the toad . . .
will not float with such a big load!

DUDE RANCH LUKE

WRITTEN BY ELIZABETH SENGEL
ILLUSTRATED BY BRIAN KARAS

Luke goes to a dude ranch.
He is a city dude.
Luke says, "I want to be a cowboy."

The dude ranch is huge.
Luke says, "There are many tall dunes.
I want to be a cowboy."

Luke pets a pony.
He feeds it a sugar cube.
Luke says, "I want to be a cowboy."

Luke sits on a mule.
He waves his hat.
Luke says, "I want to be a cowboy."

Luke feeds the sheep.
They are so cute.
Luke says, "I want to be a cowboy."

Luke uses a rope.
He makes a lasso.
Luke says, "I want to be a cowboy."

Luke sits by the fire.
He sings cowboy tunes.
Luke says, "I want to be a cowboy."

Luke is still a city dude.
But he will be back next June.
Luke says, "Now, I am a cowboy, too."

A Huge Smile

Written by Mark Day

Judy and Trudy are best friends.
Judy and Trudy have lots of fun.

Judy likes to make Trudy smile.
Judy puts on a hat with blue plumes.

Judy looks cute with the blue plumes.
This does not make Trudy smile.

Judy gets a long flute.
Judy plays a silly tune.

Judy looks cute with the flute.
This makes Trudy smile a bit.

Judy makes a house with cubes.
Judy uses the house to hide.

Judy looks cute in the cube house.
This makes Trudy smile a bit more.

The cube house falls down.
Judy has a huge smile.
This gives Trudy a huge smile, too!

Meet Sue, the T. REX WONDER!

Meet Sue! Sue is a Tyrannosaurus rex (tuh RAN uh sor us REX). Sue is a dinosaur that lived long ago. She is named for the person who **discovered** her bones. Sue's bones give clues about the past.

Facts About Sue				
Height	Length	Head	Weight	Age
13 feet high	42 feet long	5 feet long	14,000 pounds	67 million years old

Looking for Clues

It is hard to find a dinosaur **skeleton** with all of its bones. That is why Sue is special. Very few of her bones are missing.

Long ago, Sue's body was buried in the ground. Over the years, her bones slowly changed into rocks. Her bones turned into **fossils**. Now scientists can look at these fossils to learn about the life of a T. rex.

Scientists carefully dug Sue's fossils out of rock.

Sue Clue 1

Sue's teeth were long and sharp. They looked like saws. Scientists looked at animals today that have the same kind of teeth. These animals bite and tear food. They eat meat. Because of this clue, scientists think that a T. rex ate meat, too.

Sue Clue 2

Scientists looked at Sue's **skull**. They saw that the eyes faced to the front. Scientists looked at animals today with the same kind of eyes. These animals can tell how far away something is. They can tell **distance**. Scientists know these animals are good hunters. Because of this clue, scientists think the T. rex was a good hunter, too.

Sue Clue 3

Scientists looked inside Sue's skull. They looked where her **brain** once was. A brain has parts to help animals see, hear, smell, taste, and feel. They found that one part of Sue's brain was very large. Scientists looked at animals today that have the same kind of brain. These animals have a good sense of smell. Because of this clue, scientists think the T. rex had a good sense of smell, too.

Scientists are still learning more about Sue and other dinosaurs like her. Sue will keep giving us clues about the past.

Baby Animals

A baby duck is a **duckling**.
It has soft feathers.

duckling

A baby kangaroo is a **joey**.
It grows in its mother's pouch.

joey

cub

A baby polar bear is a **cub**.
It is born in a snow den.

A baby crocodile is a **crocklet**.
Its mother holds it in her mouth.

crocklet

What Can It Be?

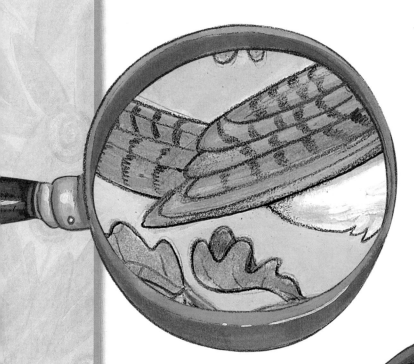

This animal is blue.
It has **wings**.
What can it be?

This animal is **gray**.
It is **furry**. What can it be?

It is a blue jay up in a tree.

It is a squirrel
up in a tree.

This animal is black and yellow.
It is **tiny**. It is buzzing.
What can it be?

The Stars and Stripes

The United States **flag** stands for
our country and for our people. It is
red, white, and blue. It makes us
feel **proud**.

Long ago, our country was small.
Our flag had 13 **stars** and 13 **stripes**.
They stood for the first 13 states.

the first flag

Our country is bigger today. Now our
flag has 50 stars. They stand for the 50
states. But our flag still has only 13 stripes.

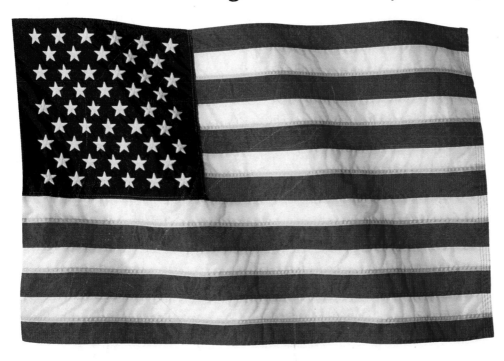

This map shows the 50 United States.

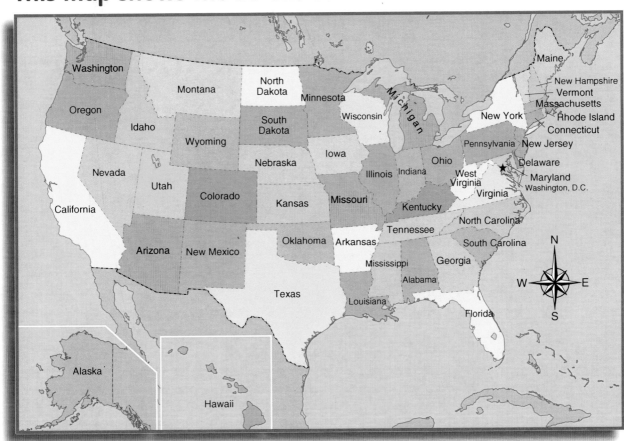

The Dog and the Bone

One day, Dog went to the **butcher** shop for a **bone**. On the way home, he went over a **bridge**. That is where everything went wrong!

Dog looked into the water. He saw another dog that had a bone. Dog wanted that bone, too.

Dog opened his mouth to get the other bone. Then he jumped at the other dog. Splash! Now Dog had nothing to eat. The water carried away his **dinner**.

The Life of a Frog

First, frogs lay their eggs in a pond. A pond is a good place because the water moves very little. Next, the eggs **hatch**. Then the young frogs eat food that they find in the pond.

frog eggs

A young frog is a **tadpole**. It swims like a fish. It has **gills** so it can **breathe** like a fish, too.

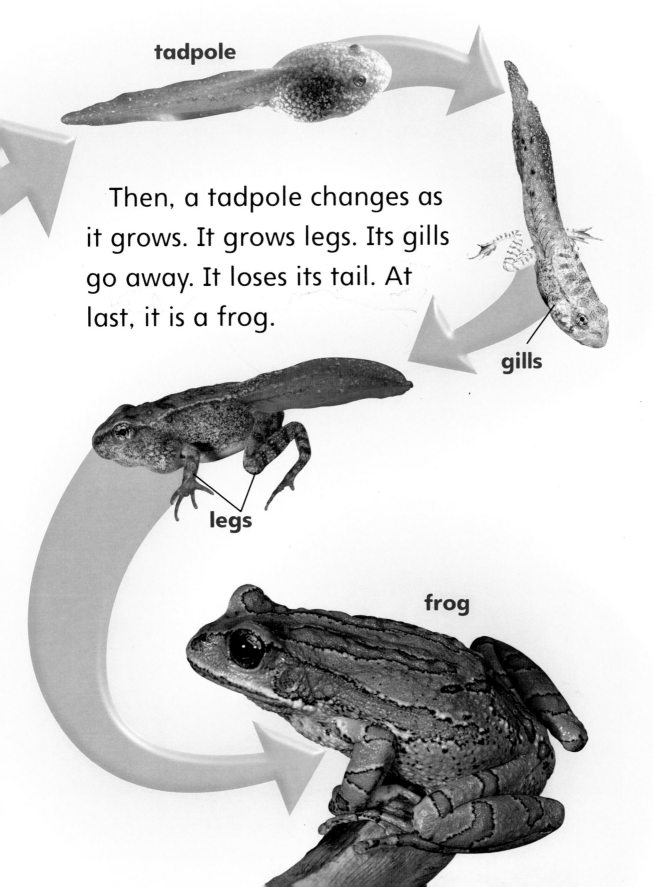

tadpole

Then, a tadpole changes as it grows. It grows legs. Its gills go away. It loses its tail. At last, it is a frog.

gills

legs

frog

The Other Story of the Three Bears

One day the three bears went for a walk. They came to the house where a girl lived. No one was home. They went in.

"What a pretty house!" they said.

Mama Bear found three hats. The first hat was too big. The second hat was too small. But the third hat was just right!

Papa Bear found three cakes. The first cake was too **sweet**. The second cake was too **dry**. But the third cake was just right!

Baby Bear found three chairs. The first chair was too **hard**. The second chair was too **soft**. But the third chair was just right!

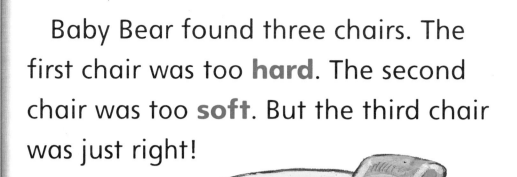

The three bears went home. Then they saw a girl run out of their house. "That girl was in our house!" said Papa Bear.

"You should not go into someone else's house!" said Mama Bear.

"It is just not right!" said Baby Bear.

Take Care of Yourself!

Exercise makes you strong.

Why should you exercise?

Exercise makes your body strong. A strong body helps you work and play. A strong body does not get sick easily. Exercise to help keep your body **healthy**.

Why should you eat right?

Your body needs **vitamins**. Vitamins help you grow and stay strong. Fruits and vegetables have many vitamins. Eat good foods to stay healthy.

Fruits and vegetables have many vitamins.

Why should you keep clean?

Germs are all over. Germs can make you sick. Soap and warm water help kill germs. Stay clean to stay healthy.

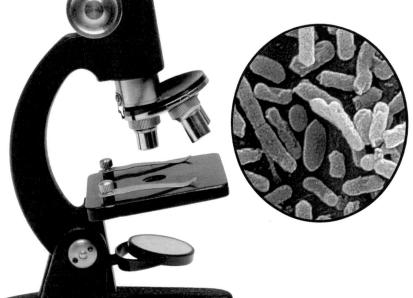

Germs can make you sick.

Sam and Bob

One **night** something woke up Sam. A little monster stood by him.

"I am going to live under your bed," it said.

Sam said, "You will be cold there. You can live in my **closet**."

Sam and the monster became **friends**.
Sam named the monster Bob.

It was nice to have Bob as a friend.
Bob played games with Sam. Bob also
helped Sam with his **homework**.

225

Sam's friend Dan came to stay one
night. "What did I hear?" Dan asked.
"Is something under your bed?"

Sam said, "Nothing is under my bed.
But my monster is in the closet."

"M-m-monster?" asked Dan.

Sam said, "Don't be scared. You
can meet him! His name is Bob."

Holidays!

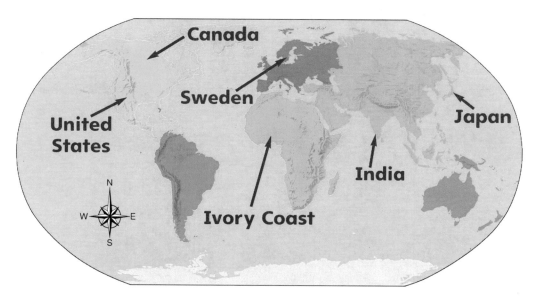

Holidays take place at any time of the year. They take place all over the **world**.

Many **countries** have holidays in fall. In Ivory Coast, people dress up and dance on this holiday.

In winter, some countries have a
snow holiday. People make ice art
on this snow holiday in Japan.

Canada also has a snow holiday.
People make ice art there, too. They
also have ice races.

This spring holiday is in India. People there throw colored powder into the air.

In summer, some people in Sweden **celebrate** the longest day of the year. They dress in costumes and play music.